Tooth Fairy

Written and illustrated by Audrey Wood

WITHDRAWN

Child's Play (International) Ltd

Ashworth Rd, Bridgemead, Swindon, SN5 7YD UK
Swindon   Auburn ME   Sydney
© 1985 M. Twinn.   Printed in Shenzhen, China
ISBN 978-0-85953-293-8   CLP290914CPL11142938
          13 15 17 19 20 18 16 14
              www.childs-play.com

Mother! Come quick! I've pulled a tooth!

Matthew, Dear. How wonderful!

Tell me about the Tooth Fairy again, please!

Every night, the Tooth Fairy flies about with her basket of goodies. Put your tooth under your pillow, and she will swap it for some treasure...

Good night, Children.
Sweet dreams.

It's not fair!
I want treasure, too!

And I'm going to get some!

But, Jessica, you know the Tooth Fairy can't swap for treasure unless you lose a tooth.

Don't worry about the Tooth Fairy.
I'll show her who's boss.

Ahhh. Just what I need. A kernel of corn.

A little paint makes it
look like a real tooth.

Tee, hee. That should
do the trick.

It won't work, Jessica.

Nighty-night, Matthew.

Jessica ... wake up!

Oh, no! I've shrunk!

Wake up, Matthew. You've shrunk, too!

Jessica! What have you done now?

Greetings, Children. I'm the Tooth Fairy.
Look what I found under your pillows.

It worked. She thinks the corn is my tooth.

Why do you swap treasure for teeth?

I'll show you. Just hold my hands and I'll say the Magic Words: "Loose Tooth Away!"

Welcome to the
Tooth Fairy's Palace!

Bridges, walls, towers,   all made of teeth.

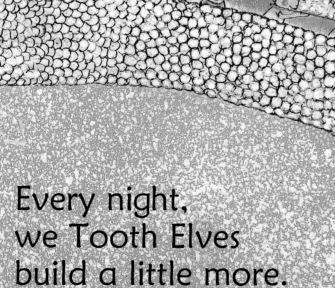

Every night,
we Tooth Elves
build a little more.

This is the Hall of Perfect Teeth.
Only the cleanest and brightest go here.

My perfect tooth!

I suppose my tooth goes here, too?

Come, Jessica! This one needs work!

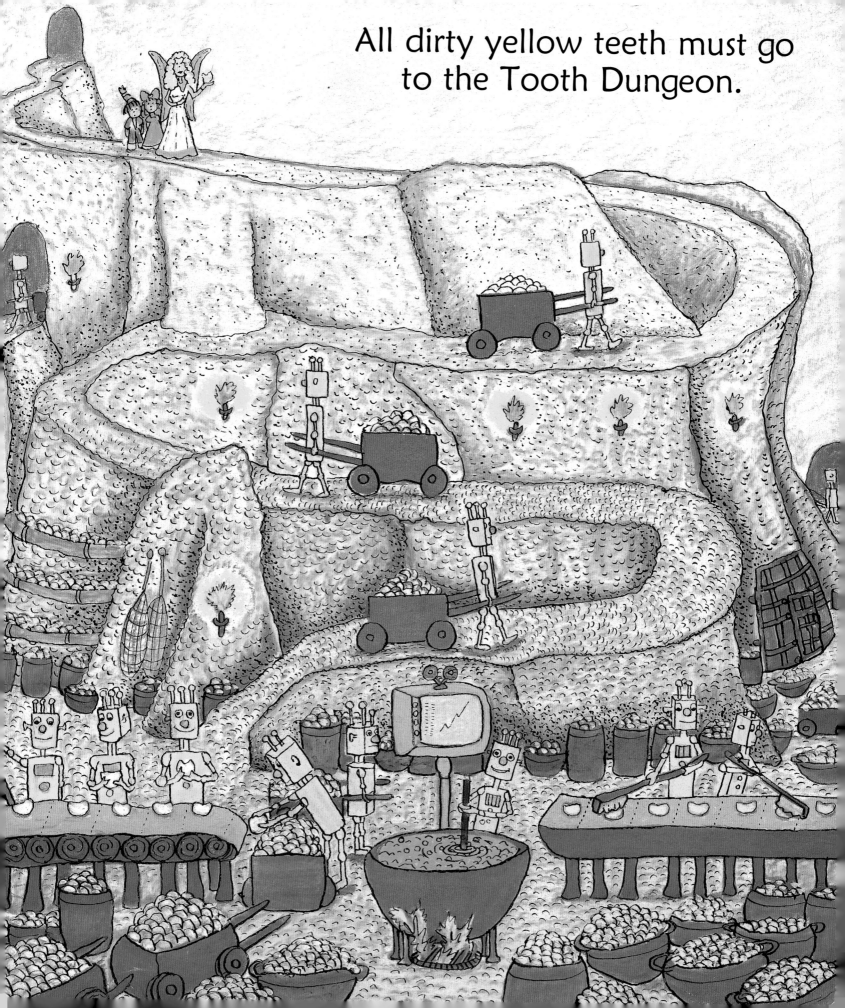

All dirty yellow teeth must go to the Tooth Dungeon.

We Robot Tooth Cleaners
boil them in the Bubbling Bath.
Then we scrub them
until they shine like stars.

Gulp!

Now we will clean Jessica's tooth.

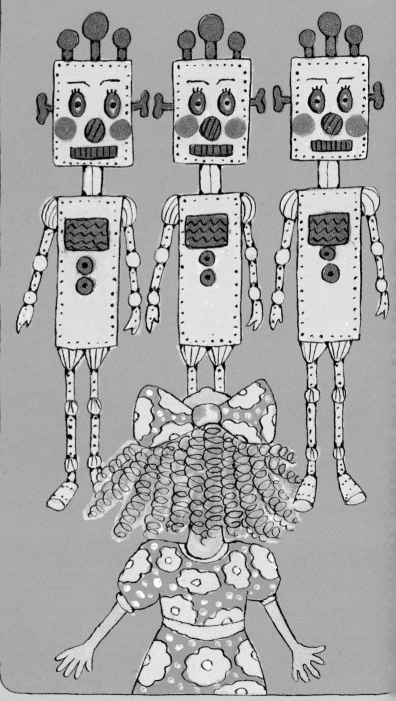

Your tooth is a fake.
We must put you
in jail.

Hurry, Children. The Robots don't like tricks.

I never should
have done it.

Cheer up, Jessica.
I'm sure you'll lose
a real tooth soon.

And you'll still swap
me treasure?

Of course.

And you'll put my tooth in the Hall of Perfect Teeth, like Matthew's?

I won't know until I see it. Goodbye, Children. Say the Magic Words as you go down the slide.

LOOSE TOOTH AWAY!

Jessica! Wake up! It's morning! The Tooth Fairy left me some treasure!

Don't be sad. Here, have a bite of my apple.

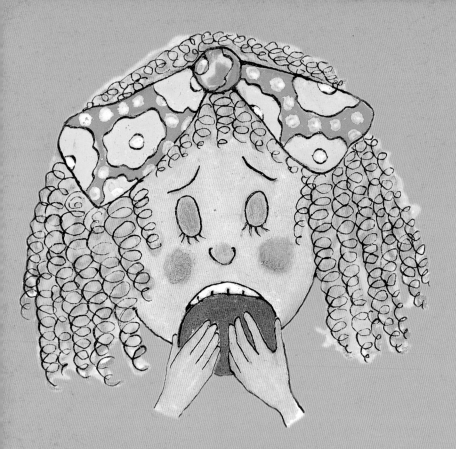

CRUNCH!

Mother! Come quick!
I've got a loose tooth!

Shall I tell you about
the Tooth Fairy again?

You don't need to, Mother. I know all about it.
This one is going to the Hall of Perfect Teeth.